D1395081

espresso
education

The Roman Treasure

Sue Graves

FRANKLIN WATTS
LONDON•SYDNEY

A fantasy story

First published in 2011 by
Franklin Watts
338 Euston Road
London NW1 3BH

Franklin Watts Australia
Level 17/207 Kent Street
Sydney NSW 2000

Text and illustration © Franklin Watts 2011

The Espresso characters are originated and
designed by Claire Underwood and Pesky Ltd.

The Espresso characters are the property of
Espresso Education Ltd.

A CIP catalogue record for this book is
available from the British Library.

ISBN: 978 1 4451 0409 6 (hbk)
ISBN: 978 1 4451 0417 1 (pbk)

Illustrations by Artful Doodlers Ltd.
Art Director: Jonathan Hair
Series Editor: Jackie Hamley
Series Designer: Matthew Lilly

Printed in China

Franklin Watts is a division of
Hachette Children's Books,
an Hachette UK company.
www.hachette.co.uk

One day, Polly and Ash
took Scrap for a walk.

As Polly bent to pick up a stick to throw, she saw a coin in the mud.

"Look," said Polly.
"It's an old coin!"

"Who is the man on the front?" said Ash.

Polly rubbed the coin to see.

Suddenly, there was a flash.
Then there came a low rumble
that grew to a loud roar.

A group of soldiers came marching towards Polly, Ash and Scrap. At the front was a man wearing a long cloak.

"Roman soldiers!" cried Ash.
A soldier on horseback rode
right past them.

"Make way for Caesar!" cried the soldier, moving them to the side.

"Hail Caesar!" cried the soldier.
"The river is not far away!"
"Good!" shouted the man.
"Call the legion forward!"

"That man must be Julius Caesar, the great Roman leader!" whispered Polly. "He was the first Roman general to invade Britain!"

17

As the soldier rode away, Scrap barked. The horse was alarmed and the soldier dropped a leather pouch.

19

Ash went to pick up the pouch. Suddenly, there was another flash.

The Roman soldiers
disappeared in an instant.

"So the man on the coin is Julius Caesar!" said Polly.

"And this is where the soldier must have dropped his pouch!" cried Ash.

"We found real Roman treasure!"
laughed Polly. "Let's see if there
is any more!"

Puzzles

Which speech bubbles
belong to Polly?

Put these sentences in order
to explain the story.

The soldiers disappeared.

Polly found a coin.

A soldier dropped a leather pouch.

Polly and Ash wanted to find more treasure.

Suddenly soldiers from the past appeared.

Answers

Polly's speech bubbles are: 1, 2

The sentence order is:
Polly found a coin.
Suddenly soldiers from the past appeared.
A soldier dropped a leather pouch.
The soldiers disappeared.
Polly and Ash wanted to find more treasure.

Espresso Connections

This book may be used in conjunction with the History area on Espresso to start a discussion on the Romans in Britain. It may also be used to inspire a creative writing activity. Here are some suggestions.

The Romans in Britain

Talk about when the Romans came to Britain – in 55BC. They stayed for 465 years until 410AD. Visit the Romans section in History 2. Open Digging up the past in the Activity arcade and ask the children to complete the activity identifying what Roman remains are made from.

Talk about how artefacts can tell us what life was like in the past. You could also consider how buildings give us evidence by looking at the video 'Important place' in Evidence of settlement.

Write your own fantasy story
Visit the Story Starts in English 1, and open Amazing story: Buried treasure. Watch the video together and ask the children what they think it would be like to discover buried treasure like this.

Visit the "Writing resource box" in English 1, and go to the Activity arcade. Choose the "Writing frame" activity and select "Story – science fiction" on the left. Tab through the information that is given about this genre.
Think about the video again – what might happen next to make it become a fantasy story? Decide on the problem(s), the events and the ending. How will the story engage the reader and allow them to escape from reality? Then perfect your class story in the writing frame, using the word bank on the left to edit and improve it.